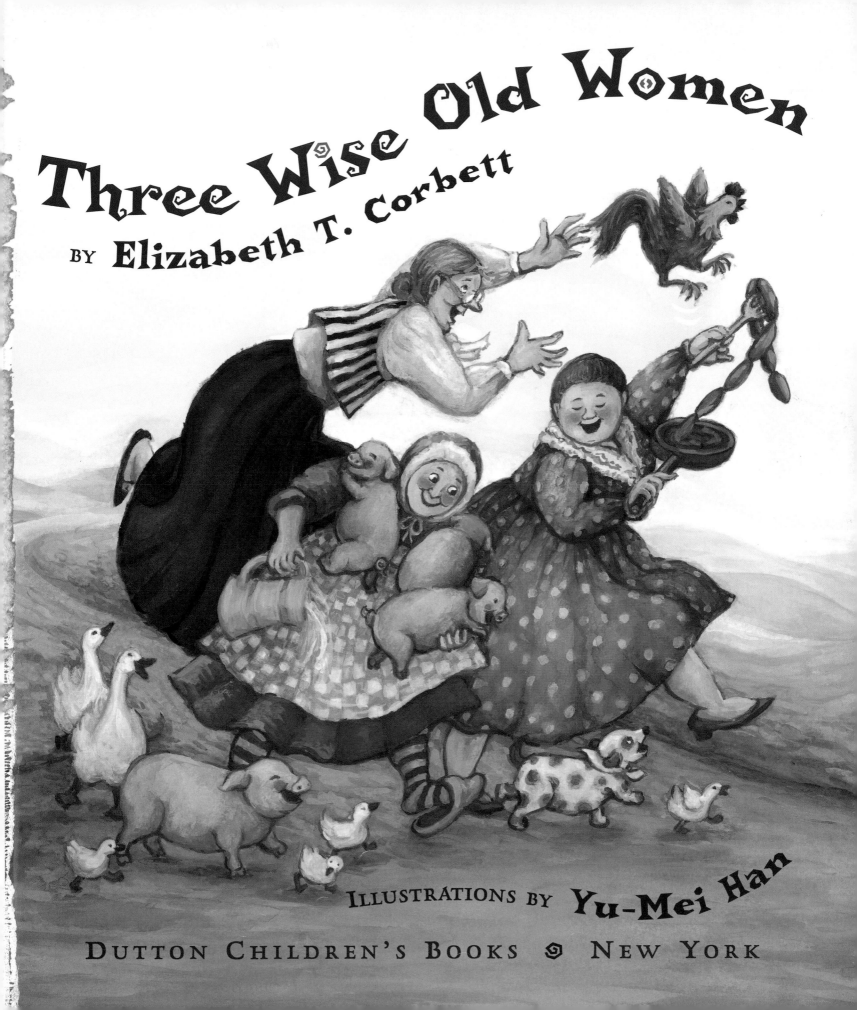

Three Wise Old Women

BY Elizabeth T. Corbett

ILLUSTRATIONS BY **Yu-Mei Han**

DUTTON CHILDREN'S BOOKS ❂ NEW YORK

Three wise old women were they, were they,

Who went to walk on a windy day;

One carried a basket to hold some berries,
One carried a ladder to climb for cherries,

The third, and she was the wisest one,
Carried a fan to keep off the sun.

But they went so far,
and they went so fast,

They quite forgot their way at last.

So one of the wise women cried in a fright,

"Suppose we should meet a bear tonight!
Suppose . . .

he should eat me!"

"And me!!"

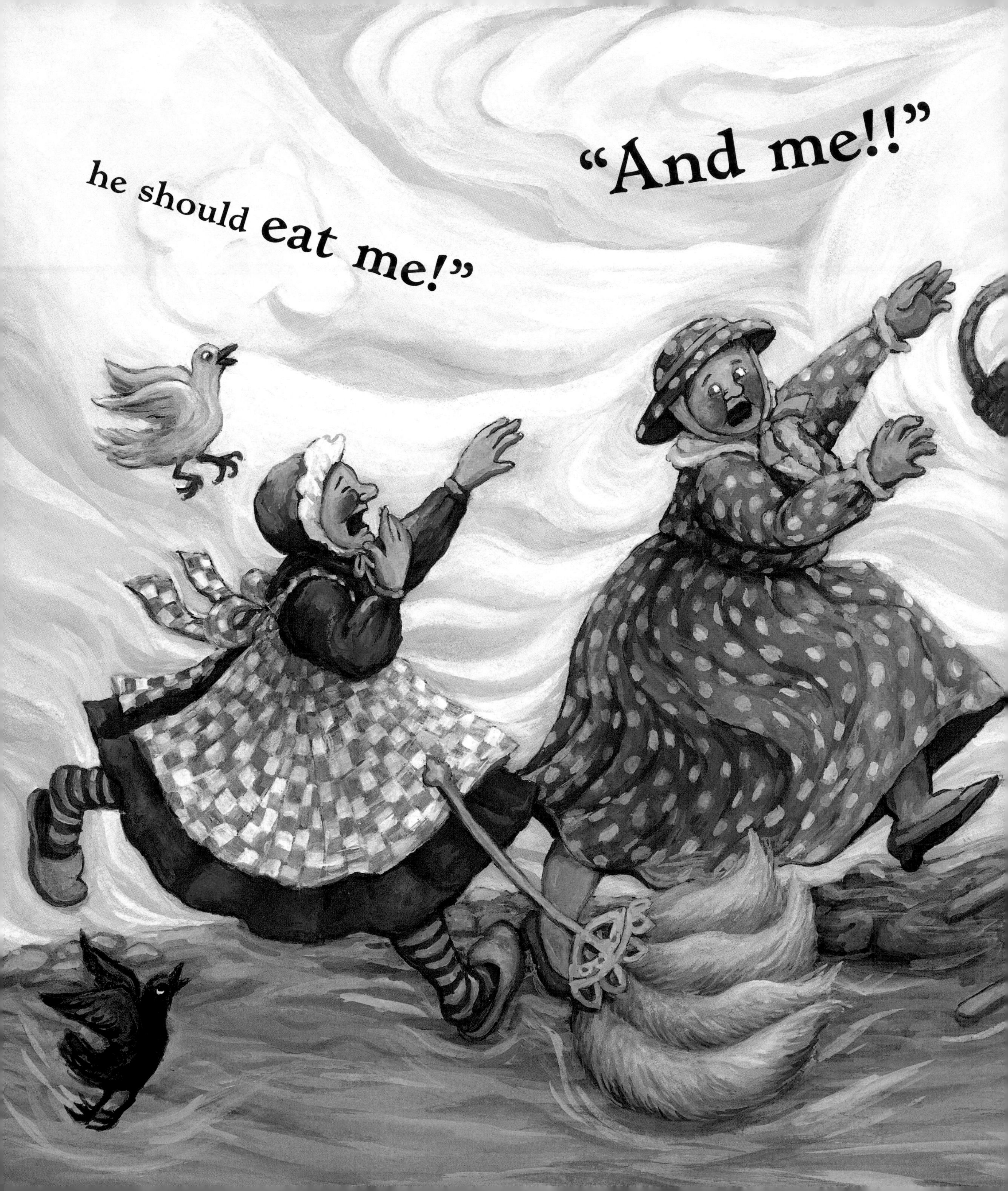

"What is to be done?" cried all the three.

But there wasn't a tree for miles around;

"Dear, dear!" said one, "we'll climb a tree,
There out of the way of the bears we'll be."

They were too frightened to stay on the ground,
So they climbed their ladder up to the top,

And sat there screaming,

“We’ll drop!

We’ll drop!”

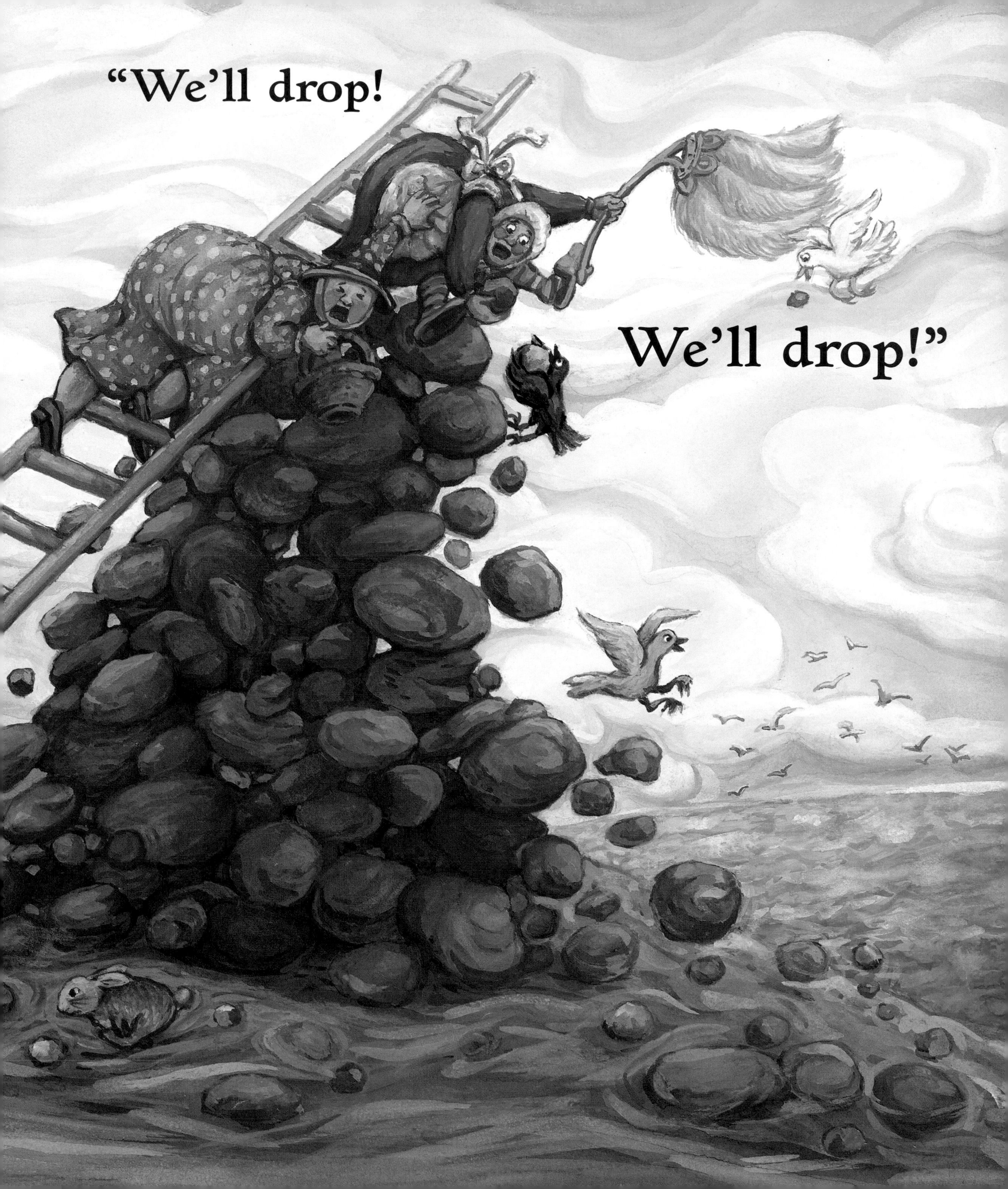

But the wind was strong as wind could be,
And blew their ladder right out to sea;

So the three wise women were all afloat
In a leaky ladder instead of a boat,

And every time the waves rolled in,
Of course the poor things were wet to the skin.

Then they took their basket, the water to bale,
They put up their fan instead of a sail;

But what became of the wise women then,

Whether they ever sailed home again,

Whether they saw any bears, or no,

You must find out,

for I don't know.

For Reverend Hsien Ming
and Reverend Ming Kuang—
thank you for your wonderful teaching
Y.·M.H.

Illustrations copyright © 2004 by Yu·Mei Han
All rights reserved.

CIP Data is available.

Published in the United States by Dutton Children's Books,
a division of Penguin Young Readers Group
345 Hudson Street, New York, New York 10014
www.penguin.com

On page 5 of this poem, the original
word *winter* was adapted to read *windy*.

Designed by Beth Herzog
Manufactured in China
First Edition
ISBN 0·525·47230·4
1 3 5 7 9 10 8 6 4 2